A.R.Quinton's
ENGLAND

THE TROUT INN, GODSTOW
UPPER THAMES

A.R.Q.

A traditional thatched cottage near Looe in Cornwall

OPPOSITE:
*The blue of distant Leith Hill in Surrey set against the
golden foliage of Ockley Green*

A.R.Quinton's ENGLAND

A PORTRAIT OF RURAL LIFE AT THE TURN OF THE CENTURY

ALAN C. JENKINS

Webb & Bower

MICHAEL JOSEPH

First published in Great Britain 1987 by
Webb & Bower (Publishers) Limited,
9 Colleton Crescent, Exeter, Devon EX2 4BY
in association with Michael Joseph Limited,
Wright's Lane, London W8 5TZ

Designed by Peter Wrigley

Production by Nick Facer/Rob Kendrew

British Library Cataloguing in Publication Data

Quinton, Alfred Robert
  A. R. Quinton's England.
  1. Quinton, Alfred Robert
  I. Title   II. Jenkins, Alan C.
  759.2   ND1942.Q/

ISBN 0-86350-187-7

Typeset in Great Britain by
Keyspools Ltd, Golborne, Warrington, Lancashire

Printed and bound in Italy by
New Interlitho SpA

ACKNOWLEDGEMENTS

The publishers would like to thank Mr Derek Salmon of J Salmon
Ltd who has made the publication of this book possible.
The extracts (including illustrations) from *The Illustrated Sporting
and Dramatic News* are reproduced by courtesy of the British
Library. The black and white illustrations on pages 13–16 are
taken from *The Cottages and the Village Life of Rural England*
(JM Dent & Sons Ltd 1912). All other black and white illustrations
except page 9 are taken from *The England of AR Quinton*
(J Salmon Ltd 1978).

CONTENTS

Bolton Abbey in Yorkshire

A glorious downland scene at the prehistoric site of
Chanctonbury Ring in West Sussex

ALFRED ROBERT QUINTON

1853–1934

Researched by his great-grandson, A. Roger Quinton

Alfred Robert Quinton was born on **23** October **1853**, the youngest of seven children and the fifth son of John and Eliza Quinton. His parents, who had married in **1840**, originally came from Suffolk; his father was born in Needham Market and his mother in Ipswich. In **1850** they moved from Ipswich to London, first to Dalston and later to Commercial Road, Peckham, where Alfred was born. John Quinton, who was both a Liberal and a staunch Congregationalist, worked on the staff of the Religious Tract Society and became Editor of the Society's publications, including *The Leisure Hour* and *The Sunday at Home*; the Society is better known for *The Boys' Own Paper* and *The Girls' Own Paper* which it also published. The influence on Quinton of his father, who did not die until March **1906** at the age of eighty-eight, was considerable, and Alfred also became a Liberal and a regular worshipper at the Congregational Church in Finchley when he settled there.

As a boy Quinton attended Hornsey School in North London. The school's headmaster was CP Newcombe whose influence was one of the main reasons for Quinton setting out on his artistic career. In July **1868**, as a prize for hard work, he presented the young Alfred, then only fourteen, with a handsome leatherbound book written by George Barnard and entitled *Drawing from Nature; a series of progressive instruction in sketching from elementary studies to finished views with* *examples from Switzerland and the Pyrenees to which are appended lectures on art delivered at Rugby School*. This Quinton kept for the rest of his life.

After studying at Heatherley's Art School he started work as an engraver in London but soon took up painting seriously. Although he later devoted himself to watercolours and black and white drawings, he first concentrated on oils, signing himself as A Quinton, and Subsequently as ARQ or AR Quinton. His last-known oil painting is dated **1885**. One of his early framed oils, that of 'Great Tangley Manor, Wonersh, Surrey', painted in about **1875**, remains with the family. Another large canvas entitled 'Above Wharfedale, Yorkshire', was exhibited at the Imperial Jubilee Exhibition at Liverpool in **1887**. From **1874** onwards Quinton was a regular exhibitor at various London societies and galleries. He first exhibited work at the Royal Academy in **1879**. This was a watercolour entitled 'At Gomshall, Surrey' and, although not a member of the Academy, Quinton's pictures subsequently appeared there with regularity; twenty in all until **1919**. In addition to this, between **1874** and **1893**, he exhibited eighteen watercolours at the Royal Society of British Artists, nine at the New Watercolour Society, later to become the Royal Institute, one at the Grosvenor Gallery, and nine at various other exhibitions.

Until **1880** Quinton's studio was at 10 Bolt Court, Fleet

Street, London, but in that year he moved to 12 New Court, Lincoln's Inn. This he shared with Henry Bailey, an artist of Quinton's age, who specialized in watercolour landscapes. Bailey's painting flourished between 1879 and 1907, and among his best works were 'The Dart at Staverton', 'Cornfield by the Sea' and 'On the Cliffs'.

As well as working in London Quinton also travelled widely throughout Europe collecting many sketches and lantern slides. He took particular pleasure in his trips to Spain in the early 1880s and it was while returning by ship from a visit to Malaga that he met his future wife, Elizabeth Annie Crompton, whom he married at Bolton, Lancashire on 20 May 1885. Annie was a descendant of Samuel Crompton, inventor of the 'mule' used for weaving. The couple went to live with Quinton's parents in Holloway before moving, after his mother's death in 1886, to 48 Fortis Green Road, East Finchley, taking with them their baby son Leonard, born on 5 March 1886, and Quinton's father. From here Quinton travelled daily by train to keep regular hours at his studio in London. In 1890 he purchased another house, lower down Fortis Green Road, and converted one room into a separate studio. However, he continued to use his New Court Studio, which his son recalled visiting in 1896, until about 1905, after which he worked solely from home. In 1891 Quinton's second son, Edgar, was born but, affected by a persistently weak heart, he died young in 1912. Not long before his death the Quintons had moved again to Westfield, Salisbury Avenue, Church End, Finchley, which was then still among fields; this large, eleven-roomed house remained with the Quinton family until 1974.

From the 1880s on Quinton was writing of his travels in England and abroad, illustrating his articles whenever possible, and slowly consolidating his reputation as an artist. 'Land's End to John o'Groats' was serialized from 4 May to 12 October 1895 in the *Illustrated Sporting and Dramatic News*, and was later published, although in less detail, in *The Leisure Hour* of 1899 and 1900. The article recounts the story of a journey undertaken on bicycles by Quinton and 'friend B' (possibly Henry Bailey) in 1894 and typifies in its text and illustrations Quinton's approach to his work. 'Our idea', he wrote, 'was to tour leisurely from end to end, to enjoy the varied scenery which our native land presents in such variety to those who care to see it, and to study the life and character which we might meet with on the road.'

This kind of journey, accompanied by a friend, was similar to many that Quinton made during his lifetime, and reflected the Victorian desire to travel and to see the world for oneself. PH Ditchfield, for whose book *The Cottages and Village Life of Rural England* (published 1912) Quinton provided seventy-one illustrations, recalled, 'We have explored together some of the quaint nooks and corners, the highways and byways, of old England, and with the pen and brush described them as they are at the present time. We have visited the peasant in the wayside cottage . . . entered the old village shop, and even taken our ease at an inn'. Quinton would be away from home for up to three months a year, staying at lodgings and farmhouses, and travelling by bicycle. He would usually work from one place for about two to three weeks at a time, and his son recalled spending enjoyable summer holidays 'on location' with his mother and father, the whole family seeing the countryside by bicycle. During the autumn, winter and spring, Quinton worked hard at Westfield in his studio, a spacious first-floor room overlooking the gardens. His paintings, now all in watercolour, were worked up from numerous photographs, sketches, and drawings produced on his travels of the previous summer. He took many of his own photographs but purchased hundreds more

Many of Quinton's watercolours were used as illustrations in magazines and books, including another of PH Ditchfield's works, *The City Companies of London and their Good Works*, published in 1904. In 1902 he illustrated articles on the Wye Valley and Wharfedale in the *Art Journal*. Of particular importance however, was a lavish book, published by Dent in 1907, entitled *The Historic Thames*. This was written by Hilaire Belloc and contained fifty-nine illustrations by Quinton. These included views of Lambeth Palace, Tower Bridge, the Houses of Parliament, Hampton Court Palace and Windsor Castle. Quinton had devoted the summers of 1905 and 1906 to work on these paintings, and the best of the originals were exhibited in 1912 at the Suffolk Street Gallery, home of the Royal Society of

British Artists. The Duke and Duchess of York bought two of these pictures for their private collection. In 1907, in addition to *The Historic Thames*, a much smaller book, *Summer Holidays* by Percy Lindley, which contained a number of illustrations by Quinton, appeared. In 1910 Methuen published *The Avon and Shakespeare Country* with thirty-five illustrations by Quinton, including pictures of Shakespeare's Birthplace, Anne Hathaway's Cottage and the Vale of Evesham. At about this time a small number of paintings were published as postcards, notably a series of village crosses by Raphael Tuck & Sons.

As well as contributing to published works Quinton was producing a large number of watercolours, many of which were commissioned and sold privately. Whereas in the 1870s and 1880s he was rarely able to sell his paintings for more than fifteen guineas apiece, by 1920 his larger pictures, approximately four feet by five feet, would fetch about one hundred guineas. He obtained some recognition for all this work when, in February 1911, he was elected a member of the Royal Society for the Encouragement of the Arts, Manufactures and Commerce.

Although he illustrated many books and booklets during the 1890s and early 1900s Quinton gained more general recognition and completed the bulk of his artistic work, in terms of pure volume, through his association with J Salmon (from 1930 J Salmon Ltd), Printers and Art Publishers of Sevenoaks, Kent, from about 1912 until his death in 1934. For most of this long period of co-operation between artist and publisher he supplied around, or in excess of, one hundred paintings a year, to a total of some two thousand originals in all. These were first reproduced and sold as postcards and many of them were also concurrently published as prints, booklets, calendars, jigsaw puzzles and other souvenir merchandise.

As a person Quinton, bearded and well known in later years for his grey Homburg hat and bunch tie, was a kindly man, purposeful yet quiet, talking little about his work. Although he could be disagreeable when angry, he was fair and strict as a father, was not a lover of socializing and had a very limited circle of friends, preferring to mix with his family. Leonard and his wife Nellie visited Westfield with their children every Sunday at

4pm for tea, and Quinton was also very close to his elder brother Ernest, the manager of a large City jewellers. He only discarded his favourite tweed jacket for occasional Royal Academy dinners and for the regular Sunday attendance at the Congregational Church where he sang with a fine bass voice. He often smoked a briar pipe, or an occasional cigar, even when working, but was not given to drinking, the infrequent whisky being taken from a porcelain decanter on the sideboard. His favourite pastimes were gardening and carpentry, and he kept a workshop where he did much of his own picture framing. He tended the large lawn, trees, and flowerbeds at Westfield with care, and so loved the peace of the garden that, so the story goes, while Leonard was away in France during the First World War, he

A colourful view of Hastings in East Sussex

An unusually immaculate cottage at the bridge, Allerford, near Porlock, Somerset

created a small flowerbed in the centre of the lawn to ensure that the lawn could no longer be used for tennis and cricket.

In his painting Quinton's particular gift was his ability to capture the flavour and colour of English rural life at the turn of the century. This he achieved, especially in his earlier watercolours, in several ways. Firstly, through his skill as a draughtsman he could reproduce accurately and in great detail the subject before him, and yet his paintings are never dull, 'photographic' images. He avoided this partly through his rich and varied use of colour, and partly through the clever manner in which he composed his pictures. He made continual use of distinctly rural elements, such as herds of cattle, flocks of sheep, horses and carts, and standing or seated figures, all of which consistently appear throughout his work, not only to bring his paintings to life, but also to suggest the air of tranquillity which he was trying to evoke. It was this ability to combine accuracy with an impression of rural harmony which made Quinton's watercolours so popular as postcards although, due mainly to the volume of work he undertook and advancing years, his later work lacks something of the original quality and freshness.

The essence of Quinton's appeal is therefore mainly nostalgic. Although he did produce many town and coastal views for postcards, he derived greatest pleasure from painting village and country scenes, thatched and half-timbered cottages being his favourite theme. In particular he was very concerned to leave a record of rural England in case it should ever be destroyed. PH Ditchfield, with whom Quinton collaborated in 1904 and 1912, wrote:

> 'Agitators are eager to pull down our old cottages and erect new ones which lack all the grace and charm of our old fashioned dwellings. It is well to catch a glimpse of rural England before the transformation comes, and to preserve a record of the beauties that for a time remain.'

Quinton's work has given pleasure to countless people largely through the many millions of postcards that have been sold, and are still sold today (and in 1981 a society was formed for collectors of these postcards). The paintings recall for us villages and countryside as they were around the turn of the century. They ensure that this vanished aspect of England will at least not be completely forgotten.

A.R. QUINTON AND J. SALMON LIMITED

The printing and publishing of coloured postcards by J Salmon Ltd, Sevenoaks, Kent, dates back to the beginning of the twentieth century and continues to this day. In 1898 Mr Joseph Salmon had inherited control of the family printing and stationery business and, mainly through a personal interest in photography, about 1900 he began tentatively to publish black and white reproductions of photographs of the Sevenoaks neighbourhood as postcards. He soon realized that coloured postcards would have greater appeal and towards the end of 1903 the first cards were issued, reproduced from watercolour paintings by the three-colour half-tone letterpress process. In 1904 an extension to the original general printing works was built in The Shambles, Sevenoaks, especially for postcard production.

Up to about 1912 various artists had been commissioned to paint pictures of their own localities and sometimes to go further afield. Although these commissions resulted in many good series, there was a lack of uniformity in the paintings, particularly when artists were working in areas with which they were unfamiliar.

It was about this time, however, that Mr Salmon while on a visit to Selfridges Store in London noticed on display in the art department some watercolour paintings of cottage and country scenes. He was immediately struck by the quality of the drawing, the clean, natural colouring and the generally pleasing effect that the artist had obtained. On examination he found that they were mainly country scenes in Worcestershire and that the artist's signature was AR Quinton. He was so impressed that he bought six of these pictures and, having made arrangements with the artist about the copyright, reproduced them as postcards. This small series proved so successful that it formed the foundation of an association between artist and publisher that lasted until Quinton's death in 1934, when he was eighty-one years of age and still painting. The exact date of the start of the association is unknown, but no Quinton illustrations appear on calendars produced by the firm before those published for 1914.

Having proved that the public liked the Quinton postcards, the problem was expansion. With some diffidence Mr Salmon asked Quinton if he would be willing to accept commissions to paint series of pictures of different holiday resorts and tourist areas, selecting scenes that would be attractive as postcards. After a little hesitation Quinton agreed to try the idea and soon a number of good series was being completed; scenic views of Eastbourne, Bournemouth, Ilfracombe, Folkestone, Dover, Lynton, Brighton and Hastings, with their surrounding areas, followed one another in quick succession.

It was soon evident that Mr Salmon could commission as much of this work as Quinton could manage to undertake and, fortunately for the publisher, Quinton was willing to give it the bulk of his time. However, the outbreak of war in 1914 with, in due course the introduction of security regulations which forbade sketching in many coastal areas, threatened to put a stop to Quinton's postcard painting. In order to prevent this it was decided to make up a programme of work in areas not subject to these restrictions. Although postcards of many of these places did not have large sales, nevertheless it ensured continuity of production until 1919 when it was possible to work freely again.

Quinton's postcard work was devoted almost entirely to scenes in England and Wales although once he did cross the border into Scotland to produce a set of twelve paintings of Edinburgh. Also there was one trip abroad when he went to Ostend in 1922 to paint a set of twelve views. On this trip he was accompanied by Mr Norman Salmon who went to take photographic views of Ostend and Bruges. Thus the association

Spring at a mill on the River Gipping near Stowmarket in Suffolk

On the right, a receipt from Quinton dated 8 February 1922, and on the left, details of final payments to Quinton's executors

thousand watercolour paintings for Salmon postcards, including 1,080 known originals between December 1921 and his death. The company holds all the receipts for Quinton's paintings from this date and these show that he was paid four pounds for each painting up to November 1922, when the fee was increased to five guineas each for most of the paintings. A lesser fee was sometimes paid if the painting did not include any figures. Also a number of originals were altered by the artist from time to time according to the changing demands of the market.

The range of Quinton's artistic skill was extraordinary. He produced paintings not only of his favourite cottages and villages but a continuous succession of all types of local-view subject matter—piers, promenades and gardens, beaches and boating lakes, castle and cathedrals, mountains and waterfalls, cliffs and harbours—any picture that was required and all in an inimitable style that raised even the most prosaic and uncompromising scene from the rut of purely representational art. In this he stood head and shoulders above artists working for other publishers in the same period, none of whom ever captured Quinton's universal appeal—many tried, but not one of them came anywhere near him.

During Quinton's long association with Mr Joseph Salmon and his company, which lasted over twenty years, there grew up a friendship between them, and Mr and Mrs Quinton made visits to Mr and Mrs Salmon at their home in Sevenoaks on a number of occasions. Both Mr Joseph Salmon and his son Mr Norman Salmon personally attended the funeral, after which they collected the final paintings from the studio. Thus was closed a unique chapter in the story of postcard publication, though the wide appreciation of Quinton's work continues undiminished through the many publications still issued by J Salmon Limited year by year.

Derek C N Salmon
Sevenoaks, 1987

continued all through the 1920s, with a slowing up after 1930, the inevitable result of Quinton's age.

A list dated 28 December 1922 details thirty-seven subjects in hand and in 1924, the peak year, an astonishing one hundred and forty-three paintings were delivered. In 1934, Quinton's last year, forty-seven commissioned works were produced, including one unfinished picture which was actually on his easel as he left it the day before he died. This last picture was a view of Sidmouth from Peak Hill in Devon (no. 4058) and was later completed by CT Howard, another artist who was working for the company at the time (and the payment to the executors was accordingly reduced by thirty shillings—as can be seen from the above illustration). In all Quinton produced approximately two

LAND'S END TO JOHN O'GROATS

PENNED AND PENCILLED BY A. R. QUINTON

PART I.—LAND'S END TO EXETER.

GOING to break the record ?" "You'll never get to the end." "How about punctures ?" These were the sort of flippant and cheerful remarks that we had to listen to from our dearest friends when we meekly mentioned that we thought of touring from Land's End to John o' Groat's.

To tell the truth, we had no designs upon the record—at least, so far as it concerns the time occupied upon the journey. The only record which concerned us was that which pen and pencil. Our idea was to tour . . . varied scenery which our . . . . . care to seek

7 min., several riders have endeavoured to wrest the laurels from Mills with varying success. Six times he has gone from end to end—five times to break a record—each time being successful. The following are the "record holders" from 1885 to the present time, as given in the "Cyclists' Year Book."

	days	hrs.	min.
1885. T. R. Marriott (solid tricycle)......	6	15	22
1886. G. P. Mills (solid ordinary)........	5	1	45

pelled to forego the pleasure of renewing our acquaintance with the grand giant cliffs and caves of old Bolerium. We could hear the restless waves beating against the rocks below ; but the armed knight, Enys Dodman, and the Longships Light-house were alike obscured from view by the drifting mist. At one mile from the Land's End Hotel our road turns sharply to the left, through the village of Sennen, with its inn, which is now no longer the "first and last house in England." The

Going to break the record? "You'll never get to the end." "How about punctures?" These were the sort of flippant and cheerful remarks that we had to listen to from our dearest friends when we meekly mentioned that we thought of touring from Land's End to John o' Groats.

THE RECORD BREAKER
ON THE ROAD

To tell the truth, we had no designs upon the record—at least so far as it concerns the time occupied upon the journey. The only record which concerned us was that which we proposed to make with pen and pencil. Our idea was to tour leisurely from end to end to enjoy the varied scenery which our native land presents in such variety to those who care to seek it and to study the life and character which we might meet with on the road. . . .

Taunton pleased us by the air of busy prosperity which pervades the principal streets, and it is not lacking in objects of interest. On our arrival the primary object of interest to us however, was lunch; and having satisfied the cravings of the inner man, we were in a congenial frame of mind to push our investigations further. The Castle first claimed our attention; it is now the headquarters of the Somerset Archaeological and Natural History Society, and contains their museum of local antiquities and other collections. My friend B. was so much

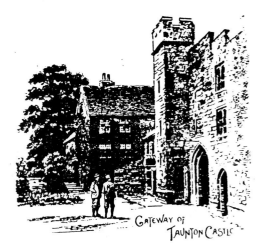

GATEWAY OF
TAUNTON CASTLE

interested in these matters that I had some difficulty in tearing him away from the company of the curator. . . .

Six miles from Worcester there is a most picturesque village called Ombersley, with a beautiful churchyard cross, as well as remains of the chancel of an old church close by the existing edifice. . .

OMBERSLEY

A few more miles, over very bumpy roads, brought us to Tarporley, our destination for the night. From a cyclist's point of view this town is chiefly notable for its cobble-stone paving, apparently of prehistoric origin. It was our first experience of this invention of the enemy, but alas! it was not to be the last. Leaving the town by Forest-road we were soon riding through fragrant pine woods, but the road was still difficult to track, owing to the absence of direction-posts, and the lack of natives from whom one could inquire. . . .

ENTERING WARRINGTON

A colliery district now lay before us; the air was full of smoke and darkness, and for the next forty miles we had rather an unhappy time of it. Lancashire is not an ideal country for the cyclist, for although nature made it beautiful, man has done his best to make it hideous. Bad roads, frightful cobbles, and noisy crowded towns and villages were what we experienced that day, and we will not dwell long on so unpromising a theme. Crossing the Ship Canal by a fine swing bridge, we entered the county of cotton and coal by Warrington, and made our way through that town as rapidly as circumstances would allow. Three miles

beyond we came upon an oasis in the desert, where Winnick Church stands upon a bank at a junction of roads; and a little beyond, where the road to Leigh and Bolton forks off to the right, there is a charming pool embowered in trees, to remind the wayfarer that the world is not all coal and smoke. Newton was gay with flags and banners, and the inhabitants were making holiday to commemorate the "crowning of the Rose Queen" in the neighbourhood. At Wigan we encountered streams of mill-hands leaving work, with clattering clogs and shawl-muffled heads. . . .

Preston is said to be one of the oldest and most beautifully situated towns in Lancashire, but we did not stop to verify these statements; certainly it has some fine public buildings, and, moreover, is celebrated for the number, elegance, and beauty of its lady bicyclists.

A CYCLISTS' RESORT GARSTANG

We reached Garstang the same evening, and put up at a well-known cyclists' resort—the Royal Oak, locally known as Mrs. Isles; nearly four hundred miles from Land's End. . .

A. R. Quinton's
England

1

In 1853, the year Alfred Robert Quinton was born, Mr Gladstone introduced his first budget. The Russians sank the Turkish fleet and invaded the Ottoman Empire, which led to the outbreak of the Crimean War. Queen Victoria permitted the physician John Snow to administer chloroform to her during the birth of Prince Leopold, thus giving rise to a revolution in medical history. Perhaps during her convalescence the queen read *Bleak House* which Charles Dickens had recently published. A social revolution was taking place in the form of the 'Railway Age', thousands of miles of permanent way spreading through the land and putting an end to the days of Mr Weller senior, the excitement of this new method of transport expressed by Turner's 'Rain, Speed and Steam' and James Thomson's

'As we rush, as we rush in the train,
The trees and the houses go wheeling back
But the starry heavens above the plain
Come flying on our track.'

And the new-fangled electric telegraph posts marched in company with the railways. An equally important revolution occurred in agriculture with the reaping-machine and presently the reaper-binder and the steam-plough making their appearance, foreshadowing the end of much rustic labour. And, so radically affecting our attitude to the whole scheme of things, when Quinton was a youth of sixteen Charles Darwin threw his bombshell of *The Origin of Species* into the midst of Victorian complacency.

Eighty-one years later in 1934 when Quinton died, Adolf Hitler had already been Chancellor of Germany for a twelve-month. France and Britain evacuated the Rhineland (only to re-occupy it eleven years later). Jean Batten had flown solo from England to Australia in the astonishing time of fourteen days twenty-three hours and forty minutes! Dr Beebe had descended in his bathysphere more than half a mile into the Pacific Ocean. The keel of the Queen Mary was laid down. In Canada the birth of the Dionne quintuplets caused a sensation long before modern fertility drugs began to be widely used. And the Second World War came one step nearer with the assassination of Chancellor Dollfuss of Austria.

Such a catalogue sums up the historic span covered by Quinton's life and illustrates the richly varied times he lived through, and the enormous changes that were taking place, affecting, for better or worse, life in the cities equally with that of the village. Yet, paradoxically, Quinton's is a world—as the Victorian age drew to a close, giving way to the sombre twentieth century and that awful cataclysm after which nothing would ever be the same again—where change does not occur, bringing to mind Rosalind's words in *As You Like It*:

'Time travels in divers paces with divers persons. I'll tell you who Time ambles withal, who Time trots withal, who Time gallops withal, and who he stands still withal . . .'.

Time assuredly didn't gallop for Quinton; it scarcely even ambled. It stood still, like some mossy sundial whose recording shadow somehow never moved. And the picture he painted of England—mainly drowsy village- and cottage-folk trudging along the rutted cart-track, but also equally slumbrous fishing-harbours—was of a tranquil, ageless scene. This scene once, superficially at least, did exist, even though behind the rose-festooned cottage walls and the dusky casements hinting at snug comfort, all was not unmitigated rural bliss—when sanitation consisted of the draughty 'house in the garden', as it was euphemistically termed, when water (heavy stuff, even with a yoke!) had to be fetched from the village well, and candles, even the humble rush-light, were the norm and oil-lamps a luxury.

Quinton was not unique; there were many artists such as he, amateur and professional. It might be mentioned here that Edith Holden of *The Country Diary of an Edwardian Lady* fame was a contemporary: Quinton often visited her Warwickshire countryside when, for example, he was working on the illustrations for *The Avon and Shakespeare Country*. All these artists were inspired by a deep love of the English countryside and its trout-ringed stream and dusky woods 'where the badger rolls at ease' and its sleepy hamlets where Rip van Winkle would have

LEEDS CASTLE, Nr MAIDSTONE

A.R.QUINTON

The grace and splendour of Leeds Castle near Maidstone
in Kent

Inn kitchens, Kent

*The light-coloured plaster and wood of these buildings in
the Loose valley near Maidstone in Kent contrasts with the
brilliant red in Quinton's other Kentish pictures*

A rust-sailed barge makes its way up the River Medway in Kent to Aylesford

The entrance to Hall Place, Leigh, near Tonbridge, Kent—perhaps Quinton passed this way when visiting Mr Salmon in Sevenoaks

felt at home. And maybe they were prompted, too, by an inner foreboding that the charm of that rural world was even then being eroded.

They sprang from a long line of painters, great and small, good and indifferent, who made a contribution to this pictorial record of the countryside and its people: George Morland, whose paintings conjure up the tang of stable and barn, the creak and jingle of harness; John Constable, especially, whose 'Hay Wain', however many times it is reproduced, evokes the essence of timeless tranquillity; David Cox, whose 'Skirt of the Forest' for instance, contains a hint of mystery beyond; Frederic Cotman (an exact contemporary of Quinton) whose often 'every-picture-tells-a-story' style nonetheless pleasingly records aspects of country life, such as in his painting 'One of the Family', with the old carthorse looking over the kitchen half-door to receive a tit-bit.

And of course those painters had their literary equivalent equally aware not only of the small, precious beauty of the English countryside but also of its transience in the face of all the pressures being increasingly exerted on it, from the demands of developers to the mechanization of agriculture and devastation of the land: Richard Jefferies, with his sometimes rhapsodic hymn to nature; Thomas Hardy, with his shrewd, humorous peasants; WH Hudson with his spare but evocative portrayal of downland and forest; George Bourne and his record of now vanished crafts; and so many more.

Maybe by implication Alfred Robert Quinton portrays an idealized world, with his charming, thatched, fairy-tale cottages fit for Hansel and Gretel, and warm, prosperous, well-found brick houses occupied by bluff yeomen. Nevertheless, it is a world many of us would love to have inhabited, contrasting as it does, from this distance, with our own restless days.

At its peak in the last century the working farming population comprised about one million and a quarter males and two hundred thousand females, amounting to one-fifth of the entire national work-force; today the proportion is two per cent. As Quinton cycled through the countryside he would have seen far

A flock of sheep passes this tile-hung, timbered cottage at Frogholt near Folkestone in Kent

*Attractive Leicester Square and its post office at Penshurst
in Kent*

OPPOSITE, ABOVE: *An imposing sixteenth-century house at
Pound's Bridge near Penshurst in Kent*

OPPOSITE, BELOW: *The old Smithy, Penshurst, Kent, with
its unusual horseshoe-shaped doorway*

The remains of a quintain at Offham, Kent

Withyham Church in Kent and a springy-turfed meadow

more people—men, women, children—working in the fields than one would encounter today. And the villages he stayed in would have been lively with work—cobbler, thatcher, saddler, cordwainer, carpenter intent on their different crafts. He would have heard the clang of hammer and anvil ringing out from the smithy amid the flash of fire and sparks, and the shriek of the huge two-handed saw as the sawyers toiled in the saw-pit—the bottom sawyer as usual having the worst of it as the sawdust showered down on his sweaty face and arms, and seen the wheelwright putting the finishing touches to a tall, proud farm-wagon, embellishing its sides as devotedly as any artist.

2

Probably half the cottages or houses in any village in the late twentieth century are owned by commuters or retired people. A minority of occupants work in or around the village they live in; many travel forty or fifty and more miles to and from their work, all the result of greater mobility. In Quinton's day most country-folk were restricted to Shanks's pony and even a visit to

A half-timbered yeoman's house at Smallhythe
near Tenterden, Kent

the market-town was an event. However for many of us the village is still a symbol of permanence, with its calmer tempo, its friendly Green Dragon or Red Lion, and that age-old token of once-unshaken and enviable belief, the village church. On these churches, through the generations, such care, devotion and skill have been lavished that often they are superbly handsome architectural monuments in their own right, quite apart from their religious significance.

In Quinton's hey-day in the last decades of the nineteenth century, there was already a growing tendency for city folk, of the more affluent kind, to move out to the country. (Had not Soames Forsyte built that sumptuous residence at Robin Hill with its cornfields and dark copses and grey-blue downs stretching unspoilt into the distance—except for the grandstand at Epsom?) The railway system had improved to standards often better than those of today; motorcars were beginning to bear their begoggled and beveiled owners through the countryside—after all, it was back in 1884 that Henry Royce had started manufacturing cars at Manchester. Apart from any new building, there were comfortable and spacious dwellings—the 'hall' and the parsonage, for example, and also the houses of thriving tradespeople and professionals. As

Red-tiled Kentish cottages on Groombridge village green

A carter with a heavy load pauses outside the mellow-bricked and tiled Crown Inn at Groombridge in Kent

The fortified end of Old Soar, Kent

*The Walks, Groombridge, Kent—not for cyclists, nevertheless this brick path must
have been a good deal more pleasant in wet weather than the majority of roads*

BUCKLAND Nr REIGATE

A.R QUINTON

A tandem of mighty working horses and the village shop
at Buckland near Reigate in Surrey

Ockley Green near Dorking in Surrey, with sheep
and a picturesque pump

BETCHWORTH, Nr REIGATE

A. R. QUINTON

ABINGER HAMMER, Nr DORKING

A. R. QUINTON

*The irregular, red-roofed cottages of Friday Street, in perfect harmony with
their surroundings on Leith Hill, Surrey*

OPPOSITE, ABOVE: *Cottages, barns and a church—three types of building, and many different
building styles—at Betchworth near Reigate in Surrey*

OPPOSITE, BELOW: *Near Dorking in Surrey is the village of Abinger Hammer, whose name comes
from the forging of iron in former times*

Early summer in the Surrey town of Dorking

A peaceful stroll along the Willow Walk at Dorking in Surrey

But the majority of country dwellings were real working-class homes, or, to put it another way, the homes of workfolk, as they called themselves, farmworkers for the most part. On some enlightened aristocratic properties, well-found estate cottages were frequently built, of good, warm brick, especially during the height of agricultural prosperity, about the time of Quinton's birth. Whole villages were sometimes owned by one landlord, with sturdy two-storeyed dwellings possessing a couple of downstairs rooms and two or three bedrooms, even a cellar and a copper and kitchen range, together with an outhouse for coal and wood.

The interior of a Surrey cottage

illustrated so alluringly by Quinton, with fine roofs and warm-looking brick walls, these are redolent of slippered ease by the hearth, the peaceful evening pipe, maybe the jug of home-brew, the purring cat in the fender. Among the population of some large and flourishing villages might be a doctor, a solicitor, architect, veterinary surgeon, farm-bailiff, saddler, wheelwright, miller, coal-merchant and so on, as well as shopkeepers such as butcher and baker, all more affluent than the generality.

And just as these occupations varied greatly, so did the buildings in a village itself, which was part of its charm. In principal many a village street was architecturally a higgledy-piggledy affair, the houses having been built at different periods and often altered or adapted during the generations. For example, many Elizabethan houses, originally constructed of timber, wattle and daub, had subsequently been strengthened by their existing walls being sandwiched between new brick walls. But all this variety was as natural as is a wood or spinney comprising many different species of trees. Village houses often 'grew' into each other just as hawthorn mingles with holly, or ash sets off oak.

But conditions varied enormously, even by the end of the century, and it is useless to pretend that they were not less than congenial for many labouring folk. George Bourne wrote of everything having to be done practically in one room, 'which was sometimes a sleeping-room, too, or say in one room and a wash house. The preparation and serving of meals, airing of clothes and the ironing of them, the washing of the children, the mending and making—how could a woman do any of it with comfort in the cramped apartment, into which, moreover, a tired and dirty man came home in the evening to eat and wash and rest, or if not to rest, then to potter in and out from garden or pigstye, treading in dirt as he came'.

And Rider Haggard (a far cry from *King Solomon's Mines*), writing in the early 1900s, declared that bad housing conditions were a major factor in the 'flight from the land' that was taking place. It wasn't only mechanization that reduced the agricultural population: 'There are dwellings that look so pretty in summer, with roses and ivy creeping about their crumbling stud work and their rotten thatch, but which often enough are scarcely fit to be inhabited by human beings. There, close at hand, perhaps conveniently placed to receive the surface drainage from the road, or even in wet times from the new-manured fields, is a pond, the local supply of drinking water.'

On the other hand, Flora Thompson in *Lark Rise* said that the village must not be thought of as a slum set down in the country. 'The inhabitants lived an open-air life; the cottages were kept clean by much scrubbing with soap and water, and doors and windows stood wide open when the weather permitted.' And she speaks of bright and cosy rooms, with dressers of crockery, cushioned chairs, gaily coloured hand-made rugs on the floor, geraniums and fuchsias on the window-sills, while in the older cottages were relics of when life had been easier for workfolk—grandfather clocks, gate-legged tables, pewter mugs hanging from the kitchen beams.

One cause of discontent was the 'tied' cottage. This prominent feature of rural life flourished chiefly after the agricultural slump of the 1870–80s, when independent workers began to disappear and regular, weekly-paid farm-labourers were more generally employed. The system was made possible by a farmer owning a cottage or cottages on or near his farm and free or virtually free tenancy would be enjoyed by the farmworker during the time he was in the farmer's employment. When, as always seems to be the case in this country, there was a chronic shortage of housing, it was an inestimable benefit for a man to have a home for his family, especially when in parts of the country a farm-labourer's wages hovered around only twelve or

The remote setting of the Keeper's Cottage, Hindhead, Surrey

*Tennyson's Lane through a lush beech wood
near Hindhead in Surrey*

VIEW FROM NEWLANDS CORNER
Nᴿ GUILDFORD

A.R.QUINTON

There is hardly a house or a road to be seen in this splendid
view from Newlands Corner near Guildford in Surrey

SHERE, Nr GUILDFORD

A.R.QUINTON

A sturdy brick-built cottage alongside the village church—
its cross topped by a weathervane—at Shere near
Guildford in Surrey

THE LONG MAN, WILMINGTON
Nr EASTBOURNE.

A.R.QUINTON

EAST DEAN
Nr EASTBOURNE

A.R.QUINTON

The brilliant russet tones of the Dorset Arms Inn and village of Hartfield, East Sussex

OPPOSITE, ABOVE: *The chalk-cut Long Man of Wilmington in East Sussex, whose date of origin is unknown—note also the farm machinery in the foreground*

OPPOSITE, BELOW: *Village crosses vary according to when and where they were built—this one is at East Dean near Eastbourne in East Sussex*

A fascinating record of the shops and shoppers at Bexhill-on-Sea's
Old Village, East Sussex

GALLEY HILL
BEXHILL

ARQ.

*You can almost feel the fresh sea breeze in this lively painting
of Galley Hill, Bexhill-on-Sea, East Sussex*

fourteen shillings a week, which, even allowing for inflation over eighty years, was exceedingly low. Incidently, during much of Quinton's lifetime, farm-wages in the Midlands and the north of England were appreciably higher than in the south because of competition for labour from industries such as the coal-mines and steel-foundries and cotton-mills.

But though a guaranteed home was of desperate importance, the tied cottage was a controversial system. It meant that a man was very much at the farmer's whim. He would hesitate to demand higher wages or even ask for necessary repairs to the cottage. He was irksomely and constantly under his master's eye and one farm-labourer was quoted as saying, 'You didn't dare utter a word as big as a clover seed or you might lose your job'.

And, lose your job and you lost your home.

The tied cottage in agriculture has always been an emotive subject; yet the principle has always existed, and still does, in many spheres of work.

*Mermaid Street, Rye, East Sussex, with its stepped cottages
and superb half-timbered Mermaid Inn*

3

The lot of the farm-labourer could be mitigated to some extent by various perks, the farmer sometimes letting him have the odd sack of flour at a cheap rate, even a flitch of bacon. There were generous beer-allowances in season, free coal for some important hands, milk, sometimes, for the children, and there was always the chance of poaching the odd rabbit, while keeping a wary eye out for the gamekeeper, an aloof character who suspected all the villagers and who was resented by them, a hostility dating back through the generations because of the harsh game-laws.

But one of the most important and most prized adjuncts to the labourer's cottage was a patch of land, either in the shape of an adjoining vegetable garden or an allotment rented from the farmer. There was sometimes a hint of jealousy in this respect: the last thing the farmer wanted was for the labourer to become an independent peasant again. There were instances, successfully sued afterwards, it has to be said, of farmers arbitrarily ploughing up a workman's garden, while the wife of one noble landowner forbade her tenants to grow certain flowers in their gardens, in case she was unable to tell whether or not anything had been stolen from the grounds of the big house.

In his humble way the labourer hankered after the land, even a quarter of an acre of it! The whole status of the ordinary countryman had been changed over the generations by the thieving enclosure acts that had proceeded at an ever increasing pace since the age of Elizabeth I. The enclosures through the centuries, including the nineteenth, largely destroyed the independence of the cottager, turning him into a wage-earner and job-seeker. In the past the common had made it possible to keep a cow for milk, butter, even cheese, and to run a few pigs. The concomitant rights such as the cutting of turf and furze for fuel in open chimney and wall-oven had enabled the cottager to cure the hams and bake bread, while in the garden itself it was worth while to grow wheat for that same bread.

So the vegetable garden became correspondingly more precious to the farmworker, summed up by the fact that one of the stated objects of the Agricultural Labourers' Union formed during the last quarter of the nineteenth century was the

The plaster and timber Saxon Cottage at Steyning in West Sussex, with its thatch like an overgrown fringe

An unusual church, famous for its Saxon tower, at Sompting, Worthing, West Sussex

The white-painted cottages of Felpham near Bognor Regis
in West Sussex

Arundel Castle in West Sussex, almost too severe for its peaceful, rural setting

*No tailored lawn for the Toddington Tea Gardens near Littlehampton in West Sussex,
but a riotous buttercup meadow*

OPPOSITE, ABOVE LEFT: *A village street at Beeding in West Sussex*

OPPOSITE, ABOVE RIGHT: *Salvington Mill, near Worthing, West Sussex*

OPPOSITE BELOW: *A working mill at Fittleworth near Petworth in West Sussex*

BEEDING SUSSEX

A.R.QUINTON

SALVINGTON MILL Nr WORTHING

FITTLEWORTH MILL

A.R.Q.

*The view from Hampstead Heath, London, would be very different today
—Quinton's married home was at Finchley nearby*

provision of gardens or allotments, and this culminated in the Allotments Act of 1882. At one time the Union's watchword was 'three acres and a cow', but that was never achieved. But the 'spud patch' (and the nineteenth-century farm-labourer depended on the potato almost as much as his Irish counterpart) was of incalculable value both materially and symbolically. Any spare time the labourer had was devoted to his cottage garden, that idealized feature of the English countryside, and it could be said that in his own fashion he worshipped far more as he wielded spade or hoe than ever he did in church, turning-to even after a long stint in the fields. 'My plot of land was no waste field either', wrote Joseph Arch in the 1890s; 'it was a fruitful garden if ever there was one, every square foot of it tilled, planted and watered, and I raised more fruit, flowers and vegetables off it than I had any use for'. And such surplus, when it arose, would be sold at the village inn (whose back-room was often by way of a shop), or taken to market by the local carrier.

Another immense advantage of having a bit of space was the possibility of keeping a pig, the traditional animal of the cottager, though in some cases where the garden was rented, the farmer mightn't allow this. Instead he might pay his workers a few pence a week for bringing along their gash and in due course dole out to them a cut of pork from his own animals. But the pig appealed economically partly because it could be kept in such a confined space, right up against the cottage very often, and partly because it was omnivorous and unfussy. Every gristly scrap or potato peeling, the tea-leaves, even the washing-up water went into the pig-swill, while the children would scour the woods to gather acorns (and armfuls of bracken for bedding). A favourite food for piggy, for he was almost a household pet in spite of his impending fate, was the waste brewery-grains delivered perhaps by the weekly carrier, for every market-town had its own flourishing brewery—especially when beer-money or beer-allowance featured in the wages of farmworkers.

Pig-killing day was by way of being a fête and it had to be done on a waxing moon, otherwise it was thought the meat might shrink. It was all still exactly like an illustration from a medieval calendar or Book of Hours. The agonized squealing of the pig touched no responsive chord in its executioners. For folk

HENLEY, Nᵉ MIDHURST

ARQUINTON

An abundance of trees almost hides from view Henley near
Midhurst in West Sussex

ROTTEN ROW, HYDE PARK, LONDON.

*Elegant townsfolk, a coach and four, even a motorcar, in this animated
painting of Rotten Row in Quinton's home city, London*

who lived on short commons during much of the year, the pig's demise meant the prospect of rich living for a while, together with the possible sale of spare meat to the neighbours. Afterwards the kitchen would be transformed into something resembling a field dressing station following on a hard-fought action, as the pig was disjointed and the housewife and her neighbours set to work preparing the hams and bacon with saltpetre, making the blood into black puddings, the chitterlings or innards into faggots and the trotters into jelly for soup, while the pig's head was kept for brawn. As they used to say in Cornwall, you could use every bit of the pig except his squeal.

Although conditions for many country-folk ninety years ago were frugal enough, at least the countryside they dwelt in and along whose winding lanes and across whose eternal fields they trudged to and fro about their work, at least all this was still largely England's green and pleasant land—in spite of Hudson's railing at the spoliation already going on. (But we had not then opened the hideous modern Pandora's Box of pesticides and insecticides and herbicides that have fouled up the land, robbing us of half our wildlife.) One of the benefits of that relatively unpolluted atmosphere was that in Quinton's time no village was without its beehives, not the factory-made constructions of

*A covered wagon stops outside Ye Olde King's Head at Chigwell in Essex
while the carter fetches water for his horses*

wood and glass and perforated metal gauze, but the traditional, age-old skep made skilfully (probably by the village skep-maker who specialized in many artefacts made of straw, including palliasses for the shepherd) of a plaited straw rope spiralled round and round into a tightly knit, weather-proof home that would house the bees for many seasons. The cottage gardens with their wallflowers and lad's love and alyssum, the meadows with their no doubt 'uneconomical' but heart-stirring patch-work of wild flowers—buttercup (''tis that that makes the cream!'), sainfoin, meadow-sweet, mullein, wild pansies, oxlips, vetches, bird's foot trefoil, campanula, agrimony, and regions such as the Vale of Evesham, with its incredible springtime panoply of fruit blosssom, or the cider orchards of Herefordshire or Devonshire, all this murmured with the industrious hum of bees, toiling through the summer days with an unparalleled devotion.

There is something wonderful and magical in the way this insignificant insect, half an inch long, can suck nectar from the loveliest flowers and transmute it, through the alchemy of its body, into a nourishing and perfectly balanced food. Although we think of sheep and goats as the first animals man domesti-cated, his association with bees is far older, even if it consisted in

CONNAUGHT WATER
EPPING FOREST

A.R QUINTON

A day out on the placid Connaught Water in
Epping Forest, Essex

THE OLD BOAR'S HEAD
BISHOPS STORTFORD

A.R.QUINTON

*The welcoming Old Boar's Head Hotel at Bishop's Stortford
in Hertfordshire—perhaps Quinton stayed here
on one of his trips*

Tranquil, but full of interest, Bray village, near
Maidenhead, Berkshire

OPPOSITE, ABOVE: *Haymaking in the Meads at Bishop's Stortford in Hertfordshire*

OPPOSITE, BELOW: *Particularly rich colours have been used in this painting of Steventon in Berkshire*

robbing the wild bees of their honey. There are cave-paintings showing primitive tribesmen doing just that. In Ancient Egypt bees were depicted on tombs and monuments. In Roman and Saxon times, honey was the principal source of sugar.

So, like their forefathers, the village beekeepers—beemasters, rather—respected, if not venerated their bees—a fact well pointed by the superstition of 'telling the bees' of a death in the family, else the bees would leave you and another member of the family would die before the year's end. The best time to tell the bees was just before the cortège was leaving the house, though in some places midnight was reckoned a fitting time. Some folk put their hives in mourning, draping strips of black crape over them.

'Maister's dead', the formula went. 'Your friend is gone. Poor maister's left us, but bees, bees, bees, please to go on working for we.'

And did Quinton, I wonder, ever hear a village beekeeper *singing* to his swarming bees to dissuade them from leaving him? They used to do that in Cornwall.

4

We have only to glance at some of Quinton's cottages to appreciate that among those working villages, one of the most active figures was the thatcher. Many of the better houses were

*A fine brick and timber house opposite a thatched cottage,
at East Hagbourne, Berkshire*

VILLAGE CROSS
EAST HAGBOURNE, BERKS

A.R.QUINTON

An ancient, slender-shafted cross at East Hagbourne in
Berkshire and the village's impressive church which dates
from the fourteenth century

*Leisurely boating on the Thames, by Sonning Bridge with
its sturdy arches*

HENLEY REGATTA

The banks—and waters—of the Thames lined with
spectators of the Henley Royal Regatta

roofed with tiles and many once thatched had been re-roofed with them, but what we look upon as the quintessential rural dwelling was thatched. In fact, up to the days of Elizabeth I thatched roofs were predominant—for barns and shippons as well and even some churches.

Gradually, thatch—despised for being a refuge for rodents and sparrows and a slummocky green-mossed sight when neglected—began to go out of fashion, to be replaced by tiles or slates or even corrugated iron. Yet thatch at its best is a marvellous insulating material, keeping a cottage warm in winter and cool in summer. Its beetling eaves can make a place dark inside, but this was not particularly important when by

and large houses were primarily shelters for sleeping and eating and little else. Well made and well maintained, the best reed thatch will last half a century, though this durability depends also on the quality of the supporting spars and sways and spicks and buckles, as they are variously called in different parts of the country, but invariably made from hazel-wood.

During the past thirty years, thatch has become fashionable again and many a ruinous dwelling has been rescued by urban refugees. There are now some eight hundred thatchers in profitable employment maintaining the roofs of an estimated fifty thousand thatched dwellings in England. The thatcher is back in business, along with the potter and the wood-turner and

ABOVE: *The White Hart Inn at Wytham near Oxford, with its
lovely honey-coloured stone and profusion of creeper*

*A cottage at Garsington near Oxford, with a familiar figure
in Quinton's paintings, the old travelling man*

OPPOSITE, BELOW: *An early village cross, to judge from its simplicity,
at Garsington, Oxfordshire*

THE BARLEY MOW INN
CLIFTON HAMPDEN, OXON.

*A convivial scene outside the Barley Mow Inn at Clifton
Hampden in Oxfordshire*

the wrought-iron craftsman, all manifestations of a reaction from a throwaway age.

It could be said that the thatcher's skill, however primitive in its origins, stems farther back than that of other crafts, for a 'roof over one's head' is essential to our existence. When, the ice age past, people gave up living in caves and took to building their dwelling-huts, these had to be roofed or 'thatched' albeit with heather or furze or turves. In the Western Isles or Connemara there are still low-built dwellings roofed in a way that has scarcely changed since primitive times. But thatch as we know it is best made from the famous Norfolk reed, produced mainly in the Wicken Fen conservation area in East Anglia; an alternative is known as Devon reed, though this in fact is produced from wheat long straw, now specially grown for thatching as the combine-harvester with its different method of cutting has brought an end to the supply of suitable straw in general. Dutch reed, too, is increasingly imported—and, horror of horrors, the plastic age has even invaded the realm of thatch!

At the same time as materials varied from region to region, so too did the styles of thatching, influenced by climatic conditions and no doubt the availability of material. In Norfolk, for example, roofs were much higher pitched and the gables sharper edged, whereas in other parts of the country, especially the west, the cottages tended to be lower, the roofs far less steep, while the thatch was often 'wrapped' right round the gable ends in the so-called pie-crust style so well illustrated by Quinton in his Oxfordshire, Worcestershire and Devonshire examples. And within regional styles, individual styles among thatchers varied, too. This could be seen in the way a thatcher would ornament the ridge or the way he would bed the thatch round the dormer windows or weave a pattern of brambles among the hazel-spars. In addition he would by preference make his own tools: the square, heavy beetle with its grooved surface for beating the 'thraves' or bundles of reed into place, the half-hooped holder of hazel-bents that could carry three separate thraves at a time; the shingling-hammer for mending the battens; and, most individual of all, his 'comb', the little rake for smoothing out the straw or reed or loosening any tangled thraves. It used to be said that a thatcher could recognize his own tools even if he were

Like the figures in Quinton's paintings, his rounded, well weathered cottages seem to fit their surroundings, as here at the unusually named Martyr's Worthy near Winchester in Hampshire

Almost too perfect, this is the Arts Guild Cottage and its tidy garden near Brockenhurst in Hampshire

*Little Jane's Cottage at Brading on the Isle of Wight—with
perhaps a prospective customer for tea*

Chestnut horses step briskly past these cottages at Ibberton,
near Blandford, Dorset

An old woman pauses to admire the gardens outside these cottages at Studland in Dorset

blindfold. And any tools he couldn't make himself, he would get the village blacksmith to make for him.

The thatcher's work was by no means confined to cottage roofs. In the days before the combine-harvester started marching across the land, corn-ricks had to be thatched, for it might be several weeks after the harvest before a farmer could obtain the services of the peripatetic threshing machine (that monster which, a generation or so before Quinton's birth, had been the cause of bitter resentment among farmworkers. Hundreds of machines were destroyed—and hundreds of 'guilty' farmlabourers deported to Botany Bay, escaping the fate of a score of their companions who were hanged).

So, when three-quarters of England's bread was home grown, the thatcher was in steady demand after the harvest. Often he would present himself at the annual hiring-fairs—which still existed in Quinton's youth—faintly degrading affairs when workers lined up like cattle to be looked over. The different workers would carry a symbol of their trade for ready identification by farmers and their wives who came to haggle for their services: the carter a piece of whipcord round his hat; the hedger would carry a bill-hook and the cowman a milking-pail; the shepherd leant on his crook; while the thatcher sported a plait of straw on his smock. The thatcher might be taken on for the season by a group of corn-growing farmers from the same area.

*Unusual rock formations and a picturesque cottage at
Ladram Bay, East Devon*

*Well known to sailors, Old Harry Rocks, Swanage,
Dorset—seen here at low tide*

One of the drawbacks of thatch was the fire hazard. With its huge quantities of reeds or straw together with the innumerable supporting laths and timber-frames, a thatched cottage was a potential tinder-box. Many villages kept special, long, hooked poles in a central place, usually the church or the church-room, for dragging off burning thatch, while it was only gradually that efficient fire-engines were evolved. Some of the early fire-fighting facilities were organized by individual insurance companies who provided their clients with distinctive plaques to fix on the front wall. There are reports, apocryphal or not, of one company's fire-fighters standing idly by while a house insured by a rival company went up in flames. But insurance was only obtained by the more well-to-do householders. Few ordinary cottagers could afford insurance, while out in the isolated villages fire-fighting was largely a matter of all hands to the bucket. Parish records are full of reports of entire streets of thatched cottages being burnt down as the result of a single errant spark.

While methods and practices in so many other trades have been transformed or disappeared—the smithy turned into a

COCKINGTON VILLAGE
TORQUAY.

A.R.QUINTON

garage, the pick-up baler making redundant legions of hay-makers, the wheelwright turning to the manufacture of car-bodies—the thatcher's methods have scarcely changed at all during the centuries. In Hardy's *The Woodlanders* we have a glimpse of Marty South making spars for thatching. Wearing leather gloves and leather apron, she worked with great speed, while 'on her left hand lay a bundle of the straight, smooth hazel rods called spar-gads, the raw material of her manufacture; on her right a heap of chips and ends—the refuse—with which the cottage fire was maintained; in front a pile of the finished articles. To produce them she took up each gad, looked critically at it from end to end, cut it to length, split it into four, and sharpened each end of the quarters with dexterous blows, which brought it to a triangular point like that of a bayonet'.

Any modern thatcher would recognize that scene.

5

Time after time one passes delightful cottages ruined today by their proximity to the road and, alas, for all the carriageways and by-passes that have been constructed, there are many villages that do not escape either.

In Quinton's day many roads were still mere tracks and it is astonishing to know some of the places he painted and see with a

A DEVONSHIRE LANE, COCKINGTON
Nʳ TORQUAY.

A.R.QUINTON

*Hefty farmhorses make their way down a lane through the South Devon countryside
near Cockington, Torquay*

OPPOSITE: *Note the 'pie-crust' thatching style here, with the thatch wrapped right round the gable ends
of these cottages at Cockington near Torquay, South Devon*

THE DART, Nᵣ GREENWAY

A.R.QUINTON

The glorious River Dart in South Devon, with its broad reaches
between rolling hills, here shown near Greenway

PLYMOUTH
NEWTON ON THE YEALM

A.R.QUINTON

The boating village of Newton Ferrers on the River Yealm
near Plymouth, South Devon, with its clusters of
bright cottages

Baker's Well, one of the deep, wooded lanes around Salcombe, South Devon — perhaps warranting one of the 'danger boards' Quinton mentions in his 'Land's End to John o' Groats' account

sinking heart what has become of them. The only traffic then consisted of the flocks being driven to pasture, the full-uddered cows meandering back to the shippon, or even a flock of geese being driven out to the village green, and the hay-wain swaying drunkenly along the honeysuckle lanes, or maybe the last of the foot-pedlars, pack on back, hoping to do business with the housewives. There was also the weekly passing of the carrier (spiritual descendant of Mr Barkis) with his hooded two-horse wagon, his passengers on the cross-benches somehow finding room between the merchandise that might be anything from crates of squawking hens, to flitches of bacon and whatnot that he was delivering to the village shop. And very occasionally, very daringly, a cyclist might swerve and bump his way along one of these secret lanes (Quinton himself maybe, why not?), scattering the ducks and hens and setting the village dogs in furious pursuit — for in the 1890s a craze for cycling seized much of the urban population, encouraged by royal patronage of Academies Set Up To Instruct In The Art of Bicycling.

But above all it was the horse that came pacing or trotting or galloping through those villages and along those lanes. The horse has played a high part in human history right back to the times, illustrated by the exciting paintings on the walls of Lascaux or Altamira, when man hunted it for its flesh. Once we learned to tame the horse, first as a draught animal, then to get our legs astride it, the horse played a revolutionary role in our lives. But though it was paramount in warfare, from the chariot-horses of Boadicea to Wellington's dragoons, of far greater significance than the glamorous beastliness of war was the horse's part in agriculture — though it was a part he shared with oxen, which were still used in a county such as Sussex as late as the 1860s.

Every village echoed with the placid thump of hooves as the horses plodded out to the fields in the mist-hung, dewy dawn, or with the gritty swish of wheels and smart clip-clop of pony or cob as the rector bustled along to visit a sick parishioner or the farmer bowled past in his varnished gig on the way to market. On many farms, especially the more affluent arable farms of southern and eastern England, the carter — or, as he was known in some regions, the horseman — was the most important

STARTBAY & BLACKPOOL SANDS
FROM STOKE FLEMING, S. DEVON

The wide sweep of South Devon's Start Bay, with
Blackpool Sands on the right

worker. This is typified by AG Street in his *Farmer's Glory* in which he recounts that at the turn of the century on his father's Wiltshire farm of about five hundred acres, no fewer than six plough teams were in constant use, with the odd general-purpose horse in addition, for which seven carters were employed. The country-wide equine population was then at a peak of three and a half million. In one county alone, Kent, there were twenty-three thousand farm horses.

The carter had a variety of jobs on the farm, depending on the season. He had to act as wagoner at times, taking pigs to market, wool to the staple, barley to the maltings, or fetching pig-meal or oil-cake. The muck had to be carted out to the fields to repay the debt to the soil that had yielded the crops. The hay had to be brought in on those topple-laden wagons, brushing with difficulty through the flower-hung droves. After the thrashing the corn-harvest had to be taken to the mill. But the most fundamental of all and the task with which the carter and his team were most associated was the ploughing, summed up by John Clare's remarking that there were hundreds of pleasant tunes and songs pertaining to the plough 'and the splashing team and the little fields of spring that have laid out the brown rest of winter and green into mirth with the sprouting grain, the

Exeter Cathedral, Devon's Mother Church, from the well tended
Bishop's Garden—Quinton was not sorry 'to get
free from the rough and muddy streets of the city' when on
his bicycling tour

songs of the skylark and the old songs and ballads that ever accompany field happiness in following the plough . . .'.

Field happiness! What a felicitous term; a measure perhaps of what we have lost.

One of the most important steps in human progress was the discovery of the way to make iron, first introduced to Britain round about **500 BC** by our first true farmers, the Celts, the so-called 'Fathers of Europe'. They were skilled ironmasters and smiths who evolved a revolutionary iron-shod plough that

changed human history. For now man had the possibility of producing more food than he needed and until there was any such surplus there could be no urban life. So the ploughman, written off as a chawbacon wearily plodding his homeward way at the tolling of the curfew, is in effect an important historic character, by implication the builder of cities from which stemmed our civilization, our arts, sciences and skills!

The carter was inordinately proud of his horses and took immense trouble in grooming them, working away with the

This painting of Lee village near Ilfracombe shows the
less-steep Devon style of thatching

A busy scene in the High Street, Clovelly, North Devon—
not a place for Quinton and his bicycle though

*The extraordinary Castle Rock at Lynton
in North Devon*

Already with hotels for tourists, this is Mars Hill at Lynmouth
in North Devon

The thickly wooded banks of the Looe River in Cornwall

wagons, forerunners of the coach (which didn't come into fashion until the mid-sixteenth century).

Then there was the Suffolk, affectionately known as Punch, a nickname expressive of its compact, muscular body under its unvarying pale chestnut coat. It was equally sweet tempered and tractable as the Shire and renowned for its long working-life. 'Horsemen' liked it also because it was clean legged, with no feathering to get caked with mud or thick with burs, no small consideration in its grooming. Tall at least as the seventeen hands of the Great Horse was the Clydesdale that could stride along with its load at an imposing five miles an hour. But it was of uncertain temper, as many a blacksmith knew to his cost.

Proudly those splendid horses paced the land, hauling the plough or the chain harrow or the swaying hay-wain or the forester's oak-trees. But though horses were still an everyday sight in Quinton's England, the villagers would pause in their cottage doorways or at the garden gate to watch the glossy teams jingling and tramping home from work, for there is always an ineffable thrill or satisfaction at the sight of a horse, not only because of its inherent beauty but because of its associations with our history.

6

Probably the most romantic country figure, in the popular imagination at least, has always been the shepherd. This was for a variety of reasons. There was the dramatic solitude of his work, making him seem like some patriarchal presence communing with the eternal as he leant on his crook watching over his flock on the lonely downs where the buzzard wheeled and the hare limped by. He brought to mind those biblical images, 'the good shepherd giveth his life for the sheep', 'rejoice with me; for I have found my sheep which was lost', and of course those fearful shepherds to whom glad tidings were brought by the shining angel. Maybe, too, in our inner consciousness, the shepherd causes us to think back to the far-off days when men turned from being merely hunters and gatherers and took to a pastoral life, the first step on the way to a true agricultural system.

curry comb and the dandy brush, coiffuring mane and tail, sponging eyes and ears. Every carter, too, had his own patent method of imparting a gloss or bloom to a horse's coat: some would even rub a horse down with a cloth that had been dipped in paraffin; others would attain their object through diet, feeding the horses dried tansy leaves or chopped bryony root; black antimony, too, was sometimes used to produce a handsome shine on those majestic equine bodies.

Indeed, they were magnificent animals. A horse such as the Shire, heaviest and largest type of horse in the world, often weighed nearly a ton and was capable of hauling a five-ton load, and nothing could be more stirring, more redolent of animal strength, than the sight of, say, three or four Shires in tandem dragging a hugely loaded timber carriage or pole wagon out of the forest. In Elizabethan times the Shire used to be known as the Great Horse of England, for in medieval times a horse of very great strength had been required to carry a knight in armour weighing altogether perhaps thirty stone. And the Shire had been used to haul the massive, cumbersome, springless

Quinton often uses blue and grey-green as foils to his autumnal tones but here in this detailed picture of Newlyn harbour, Cornwall, they take first place

THE OLD MILL DUNSTER

A.R.QUINTON

*Mellow brick, stone and plaster blend into the encroaching
greenery at the Old Mill, Dunster, Somerset*

OPPOSITE, ABOVE: *A superbly executed study of a fine boat
at the quay, Minehead, Somerset*

OPPOSITE, BELOW: *The thatch looks a little sparse on these pretty
cottages at Carhampton, Somerset*

THE QUAY, MINEHEAD

A.R.QUINTON

CARHAMPTON, SOMERSET

A.R.QUINTON

And there was something else, something mysterious about that solitary figure of the hills. This was hinted at in the race-memory, as we might call it, by the fact that until a century or two ago in certain upland districts of the country, the shepherd even used Celtic numerals for counting his sheep—yan, tan, tethera, methera, pimp, sethera, lethera, hovera, dovera, dick—and it was claimed by Elizabeth Mary Wright in her *Rustic Speech and Folk-lore* (**1913**) that this might be:

'. . . a curious link with our Celtic predecessors, coming down as it does so near our own times. Our Anglo-Saxon forefathers never amalgamated with the Celts, and the Celtic language never seriously influenced English. The Celtic loan-words borrowed by the Anglo-Saxons are comparatively few, chiefly names of places and things of no special importance. From a linguistic point of view it is strange to find such an everyday implement as a set of numerals persisting in the spoken speech of a people who hardly knew another word of the language of which these formed part, and who of course had their own numerals. It is perhaps not too romantic an explanation to suggest that among the few Celts who became subjects to the foreign invaders were the humble shepherds who had always tended sheep on the north country moors and fells. The new settlers would doubtless find it useful to keep them on in their hereditary occupation, and in taking over

Children fishing and a welcoming thatched cottage make up this idyllic scene at Brandish Street near Porlock, Somerset

The cross, Crowcombe, Somerset

The bleaker hills of Exmoor encircle Lorna Doone Farm
near Malmsmead

Draught horses below the spectacular Lion Rock
at Cheddar village, Somerset

the shepherd, they also took over his system of numeration, which in his mind was indissolubly associated with the sheep under his care . . .'.

For me, at least, that is a fascinating thought, for though we in this brash age think everything started at our special behest, invention, volition, our past and present are immutably connected and continuous; the shadows of the past still touch us even though they are sometimes rendered faint by all the modern glare.

However, aside from all this, the shepherd was respected for very practical reasons. For the farmer he was a highly valued worker who could be relied on entirely and whose advice was often sought even on matters unrelated to his immediate calling. For the contemplative side of the shepherd's work did help to increase his experience and mature his judgement. He could, however, as a result be an uncomfortably independent character at times, harbouring his own rigid ideas about sheep-farming— the rotation of pasture, for example, the additional feed necessary, such as roots and kale, and when to sell the 'cast' ewes, when to shear. This autocratic tendency is well pointed, by AG Street again, in his account of a Wiltshire shepherd who threatened to quit the neighouring farm where he was employed because the farmer had failed to consult him over the question of selling a spare stack of hay!

And yet, in Quinton's England, a shepherd was often paid between eleven and thirteen shilling a week, not the best instance, one would have thought, of the hire being worthy of the labour—and incidentally the shepherd, like the carter and the cowman, continued to be hired by the year. True, he was

*The golf links on Cleeve Hill near Cheltenham,
Gloucestershire, with a classic English landscape in the
distance*

VILLAGE CROSS
RIPPLE, NR TEWKESBURY

A.R.Q.

The slender village cross at Ripple, near Tewkesbury,
Gloucestershire

The Market House, Chipping Campden, Gloucestershire

Prosperous Tewkesbury in Gloucestershire, with its buildings from many different ages and its King John's Bridge over the Avon— 'a delightful place' according to Quinton

always considered first when a cottage became available, and if there was no accommodation he would receive an additional two shillings a week, together with one pound a year fuel allowance. As for his work, a penny for each lamb reared was paid in many districts at the turn of the century, and a whole sixpence for 'doubles' or twins, while the going rate for every hundred sheep that were shorn was thirteen shillings. Meanwhile, his wife was probably paying about six shillings a week for bread and flour for the family, one shilling and threepence for bacon and sixpence for sugar.

To that catalogue of reasons for romanticizing the shepherd could be added certain key aspects of his work. Not least in this respect, the shepherd conjured up visions of lambing-time, that joyful manifestion of life's renewal, with the lambs (we like to think) the symbol of innocence as they 'frisk i' the sun' and run races and put on their spring-heeled antics. Apart from the help of motor-transport and sometimes a motorized caravan instead of the corrugated-iron wheeled hut at lambing-time, shepherding has changed far less than any other aspect of farming: combine-harvesters and rotating milking-parlours have no equivalent in the business of helping a ewe deliver her lambs! At certain seasons, the shepherd's was (and is) a concentrated, exacting task, lambing-time the most strenuous of all, when some shepherds could say that for weeks on end they never took off their clothes, their work and vigil proceeding day and night. Within the straw and sack-padded hurdles up on the lonely heights the shepherd would make his constant rounds, his lantern bobbing here and there so that folk down in the village going to bed would observe that 'Shepherd's at his work again!'. There would be no proper sleep for the shepherd; all he could do was to snatch a brief half-hour or so on a makeshift pallet of straw and sacks in the wheeled hut hauled up by the farmer's work-horses in anticipation of the lambing-season. And every now and then the shepherd's wife or children would bring him up his dinner to relieve the monotony of bread and cheese on which he chiefly existed. And later on, when the time came for docking the tails of the lambs, those tails would be the shepherd's perks, for they made a rich pie that was greatly valued!

But if ever there was job-satisfaction (as modern jargon has

COOMBE BISSETT
NR SALISBURY

A.R.QUINTON

*Cattle lumber over the bridge at Coombe Bissett
near Salisbury, Wiltshire*

*A magnificent beech and a cluster of cottages fringe the Avon
at Lake near Salisbury, Wiltshire*

*Quinton's countrymen and women seem to spring naturally
from their surroundings, here at Castle Combe, Wiltshire*

it) the shepherd certainly enjoyed it. He could have said with Corin in *As You Like it*:

> 'Sir, I am a true labourer: I earn that I eat, get that I wear, owe no man hate, envy no man's happiness, glad of any man's good, content with my harm: and the greatest of my pride is to see my ewes graze and my lambs suck'.

Yet if lambing-time was necessarily a lonely job, the shearing was in loud contrast. Like Corin again, the shepherd could say 'But I am shepherd to another man and do not shear the fleeces that I graze', though he would assuredly oversee the work. Many hands were needed for the shearing in days when no such things as electric clippers existed and the work was far slower than the few minutes a modern shearer needs for each sheep. The sheep-shearing scene had not changed since the vignettes depicted in the fourteenth-century *Shepherd's Calendar* in the British Museum. In isolated regions neighbours would combine to help with each other's work, otherwise professional gangs would be hired. In either case, the ovine equivalent of the harvest used to be the occasion for a feast, accompanied by sheep-shearing songs and pastoral revelry under the command of an elected king or queen of the shearers.

At the shearing of each sheep an astonishing transformation was enacted. Who better to describe it than Thomas Hardy, whose Gabriel Oak was a prototype among shepherds—and whose story Quinton must surely have read, appearing as it did when he was a young man:

> 'The clean, sleek creature arose from its fleece—how perfectly like Aphrodite rising from the foam should have been seen to be realized—looking startled and shy at the loss of its garment, which lay on the floor in one soft cloud, united throughout, the portion visible being the inner surface only, which never before exposed was white as snow, and without flaw or blemish of the minutest kind . . .'.

Very nice, too, though I must say I never envisaged Aphrodite, alias Venus, looking like a sheep. Nevertheless that fleece was a golden fleece indeed and is another reason why the shepherd was such an historic and respected figure. For, still symbolized by the woolsack on which the Lord Chancellor squats, wool was the basis of England's wealth and prosperity in the Middle Ages.

From Norman times England had been a great sheep-breeding country and this reached its climax in the fifteenth century when foreign visitors used to marvel at the number of sheep, kept by the abbeys and sheep-barons and rich farmers—though it has to be said that this was often achieved at a brutal price. During the Tudor dynasty, for example, tens of thousands of acres were turned over to sheep-farming, entire villages destroyed to make room, and once-independent peasants were turned into vagabonds. It was a social phenomenon paralleled by the Highland clearances of the eighteenth and nineteenth centuries.

But some regions, such as the Cotswolds whose wool was boasted as the finest in Europe, and some people, benefited. Many of the handsome stone farmhouses and fulling-mills and the splendid churches that Quinton visited owed their existence to those golden fleeces and the shepherds who watched their flocks by night and by day.

7

Looking at Quinton's cottages and houses, one is bound to speculate about the women who lived in them and the families they brought up. Some of course were in comfortable circumstances, made evident by those spruce, solid-looking houses (what a splendid place Great Tangley Manor must have been, the subject of Quinton's last oil painting in 1875 before he turned over to watercolours). There were the ladies of professional men such as doctors or solicitors who had by now often moved out to the villages or the wives of well-to-do tradesmen such as the wheelwright or miller and the many yeomen-farmers who had weathered the depression of the 1870s. *And* there was always the parson's wife who in all her varied forms has been so well portrayed by Trollope. Many did good works (as did the wife of the squire or the aristocratic landowner) doling out blankets or cast-off clothes or even soup and bread and a little coal to indigent or aged villagers, though some of those ladies tended to be autocratic as to the way the generality of folk should comport themselves, particularly children—and in

One of the village crosses, which so interested Quinton,
here seen at Castle Combe in Wiltshire

Tranquil reflections at Hampton Ferry, near Evesham,
Worcestershire

*The glorious panorama of the Vale of Evesham and the River Avon
in Worcestershire*

AT HARVINGTON Nʳ EVESHAM

A.R.QUINTON

The beetling eaves of this cottage at Harvington near Evesham
in Worcestershire must have made it dark inside

OPPOSITE: *The River Avon slips under the Old Bridge*
at Pershore in Worcestershire

church farm-labourers and their families sat at a discreet distance from 'the quality'.

But for many of the workfolk wives, life was often a fair old grind, scrimping and scraping to keep a family clothed and fed on the husband's wages of a good deal less than one pound a week. 'The ordinary breakfast', wrote Joseph Arch, 'would be a tea-kettle broth—that is, bread in an all-purpose cooking-pot with hot water poured on it; for dinner there would be a few potatoes, some bread, and occasionally a bit of bacon, but the bacon was most often seen on the father's plate while the rest had to feed on the smell of it; then for supper bread again and perhaps a small bit of cheese. Here was high living for a working-man!'

Swedes and turnips were a great standby, sparrow-pie was no fiction, though some folk preferred blackbirds, as being bigger; tea was taking the place of home-brew when it could be afforded but, oddly enough, even in dairy regions, farmworkers and their families didn't drink much milk. Hardy's dairyman Crick said: ''Tis what I hain't touched for years— not I. Rot the stuff; it would lie in my innerds like lead'. It was remarked in the last century that families in Scotland drank more milk than their English counterparts and that their children were healthier as a result.

There were many modest ways of easing conditions. As we have seen, the cottage garden was of vital importance and this and keeping a pig was the joint responsibility of husband and

VILLAGE CROSS. WYRE
Nᴿ EVESHAM

The heart of a living, working village: Wyre near Pershore, Worcestershire

wife. Many wives would make pies for sale or take in laundry, particularly useful when there were middle-class families in the neighbourhood. In many villages there were friendly societies or benefit clubs (and pig clubs and coal clubs) to which the wife would subscribe what pennies could be spared, against death and sickness. But, owing to the ignorance and illiteracy of the members, control of these clubs sometimes got into the hands of unscrupulous types, exemplified by Hudson's Elijah Raven who so heartlessly swindled the Winterbourne Bishop club.

But the prototype picture of the farm-labourer's wife was of someone in a starched sun-bonnet among the hay-stooks or the corn-sheaves. It was at the hay-making and harvest-time—

especially the latter—that a man's wife was additionally valuable, raking, binding, stooking. In the more prosperous times, many farmers would refuse to take on a new man unless he had a wife and son who could help with the work. But, apart from the extra financial gains at harvest-time, one of the most valuable perks for the workfolk wife was the gleanings most farmers allowed after the corn-harvest. The importance of this perk was indicated by the fact that in some districts a special gleaner's bell was rung to signal the permitted time to start and finish gleaning for the day; no woman was allowed to start gleaning before the morning bell, nor continue in the fields after the evening bell.

*One of Quinton's finest and most typical paintings, Wyre village,
near Pershore in Worcestershire*

A well kept Cotswold-stone row at Broadway in Worcestershire

The gleaning was hard labour, made more acute because the women were competing with one another for the spilled grain. 'Up and down and over and over the stubble they hurried', Flora Thomspson wrote in her classic description of 'leazing', as it was called locally, 'backs bent, eyes on the ground, one hand outstretched to pick up the ears, the other resting on the small of the back with the "handful". When this had been completed, it was bound round with a wisp of straw and erected with the others in a double rank, like the harvesters erected their sheaves in shocks, besides the leazer's water-can and dinner-basket'.

It's a scene straight out of Corot or Millet! But the single ears increased into a sizeable load, carried home in triumph on the woman's head. In good times, gleaning lasted a couple of weeks, at the end of which the corn would be thrashed with the flail at home, then taken to the miller, resulting in maybe a bushel or two of flour for home-baked bread.

One of the most romanticized of women's jobs used to be in the dairy—the attitude to which had long ago, in the early seventeenth century, been expressed by Sir Thomas Overbury's *A Fair and Happy Milk-maid* 'who was a Country Wench, that is so far from making herself beautiful by art, that one look of hers is able to put all face-physic out of countenance. In milking a Cow, and straining the teats through her fingers, it seems that so sweet a milk-press makes the milk the whiter or sweeter'.

A variety of cottages at Cropthorne in Worcestershire

Nevertheless, even though the milkmaid or dairy-woman worked extremely long hours, rising before dawn and going to bed as 'the beetle wheels his droning flight', and had to be skilled not only in milking but also in skimming milk and making butter and cheese, it was an infinitely pleasanter job than some other farmwork women did. For example, this scene from Hardy's *Tess of the d'Urbervilles* (published when Quinton was thirty-eight):

'The dairymaids and men had flocked down from their cottages and out of the dairy-house with the arrival of the cows from the meads, the maids working in pattens, not on account of the weather, but to keep their shoes above the mulch of the barton.

Each girl sat down on her three-legged stool, her face sideways, her right cheek resting against the cow. After Tess had settled down to her first cow there was for a time no talk in the barton, and not a sound interfered with the purr of the milk jets into numerous pails . . .'.

Contrast that with the work carried out when the use of ice for east-coast trawlers became widespread before the general use of refrigeration. Thousands of country-women and children were employed, perforce during the coldest weather. Wherever there were suitable marshes or fields that could be deliberately flooded for the purpose in Lincolnshire, Norfolk, Essex, the women went stooping and shivering along, picking up the ice with their

A cottage garden in full bloom at Elmley Castle, Worcestershire

A steeply thatched Worcestershire house at the village cross, Ashton-under-Hill

naked fingers. The ice was sold by the cartload to trawlermen and the fish-trade in general. The business was so lucrative that many farmers regarded ice as a crop. When cold weather threatened, they would post farm-hands to report when the ice began to form, in order to protect it against skaters, or theft by neighbouring farmers.

The straitened circumstances of many country workfolk naturally affected the attitude to children and their capacity for work. All children were considered capable of some farmwork, however insignificant—stone-picking, stripping osiers for basket-making, collecting acorns for pigs, gathering cockles in coastal districts, bird-scaring. In Hudson's *A Shepherd's Life* there is a poignant vignette of a small boy running half a mile across the fields just to see Hudson walk past, 'because the job was so lonesome'.

But as children grew older a division occurred. Boys of workfolk families were expected and encouraged to remain at home, for they were soon at an age to earn more than the occasional pennies. However, once compulsory education was introduced, this work was curtailed, a mixed blessing for many families for whom even a boy's scanty earnings mattered.

ELMLEY CASTLE, WORCS.

An incongruous sight today—sheep being driven through a village:
Elmley Castle, Worcestershire

*Goodrich Castle, almost hidden by a dense belt of trees,
above the River Wye, near Ross, Herefordshire*

*The fascinating Old Market Hall at Ledbury
in Herefordshire*

Occasionally we get a typical and evocative glimpse of children at work, such as this one from Arthur Gibbs in the 1890s:

'In the fields beyond the river haymakers are busy with the second crop. Down to the ford comes a great yellow hay-cart, drawn by two strong horses, tandem fashion. One small boy alone is leading the big horses. Arriving at the ford, he jumps on the leader's back and rides him through. The horses strain and "scaut" and the cart bumps over the deep ruts, nearly upsetting. Luckily there is no accident. So much is entrusted to these little farm lads, it is a wonder they do the work so well'.

However, a girl reaching her teens meant complications. When she was a child she too could help in a multitude of farm-chores and all the children of a family could and often did, of necessity, sleep in one bedroom. But once a girl reached a certain age she was not only of less financial gain than a boy, at least as far as farmwork was concerned, but she also upset the sleeping arrangements in a cottage that rarely contained more than two bedrooms. What's more, she still had to be fed!

She wasn't exactly pushed out of the nest, but was more or less told it was time she 'got a place'. There were various 'craft' outlets for girls (and of course for women), such as lace-making and glove-making and especially straw-plaiting. All these had previously been flourishing cottage-industries but now tended to be carried out in small factories. In counties such as Bedfordshire, thousands of girls were thus employed, mostly at straw-plaiting as straw was in great demand for making bags and baskets and hats and bonnets. But one of the favourite, even most coveted jobs for a village girl of a labouring family was in domestic service. According to Flora Thompson, the first situation was known as a 'petty place', perhaps in the household of a wheelwright or schoolmaster or farm-bailiff. It was paid a mere shilling a week, but was regarded as a stepping-stone to higher things and was always for a twelve-month stint. Most employers treated a girl as a member of the family and with good and abundant food an adolescent had the chance not only of gaining experience but of living in far better conditions than at home. And after the 'petty place' there was the hoped-for 'gentleman's service', while the growing influx of middle-class 'carriage-folk' into the countryside increased the possibilities.

*The River Wye in Herefordshire, with Hay-on-Wye in the
folds of the hills*

LUDLOW, FROM THE HILL

A detailed and vibrant portrait of Ludlow in Shropshire,
from the Hill

There is a wistful mood to this picture of the ford, Wixford,
near Stratford-upon-Avon, Warwickshire, at evening

LEFT:
*A timeless yet intimate scene at the Mill,
Welford-on-Avon, Warwickshire*

Anne Hathaway's cottage, Shottery, Warwickshire

LEFT:
*Two sturdy working horses make their way back to an old
farmhouse at Welford-on-Avon in Warwickshire, here
seen in spring*

*Caught in mid-step, as if in a photograph, a woman crosses Warwick's Mill Lane
with its lovely row of mellow, half-timbered cottages*

TARVIN, Nᴿ CHESTER

Intricate timbering on Cheshire cottages at Tarvin near Chester

The poignant difference between a girl's home conditions and those she went to on taking up service with a middle-class family is comically summed up by George Bourne:

> 'The state of the cottages is betrayed naively by the young girls who go from them into domestic service. "You don't seem to like things sticky", one of those girls observed to a mistress distressed by sticky door-handles one day and sticky table-knives the next day. That remark which Richard Jefferies heard a mother address to her daughter, "Gawd help the poor missus as gets hold of *you!*" might very well be applied to many and many a child of fourteen in this valley, going out, all untrained, to her first "place" . . .'.

8

There used to be an old song that went something like 'O this is the crown of the year, Heigh-ho the harvesting time!'. Nowadays the harvest is perhaps largely taken for granted and the modern harvest is more like a scene from some outdoor factory, with monstrous machines waddling across the land, reaping, thrashing, spewing out the grain all in one, the equivalent of factory chimneys being the subsequent rolling clouds of smoke from stubble fires.

But in Quinton's day the harvest was truly the crown of the

*Craggy Topley Pike and a stream, near Buxton in
Derbyshire, with a hay-cart below*

year. There was still that atavistic feeling for everything the
harvest meant, a throwback to the time when a good harvest or
a bad was the difference between ease and plenty—and hard
commons, if not starvation. Even nowadays few sights are more
satisfying or thrilling than a rolling field of ripe wheat, stirring in
the breeze, gleaming gold in the sun. But in the days we are
talking about there was more actual physical contact with the
earth. Even the horse-drawn mechanical reaper (which, with its
red arms whirling, looked like a grotesque version of one of Don
Quixote's windmills), introduced in mid-century, still required
many workers to rake and stook the corn out of the way so that
the jingling team could come plodding back downfield. In any
case, for many years afterwards, much of the harvest was still
accomplished with sickle and scythe and there was sometimes
the spectacle of labourers bent at their task on one farm while
across the hedge on a neighbouring property the mechanical
reaper clattered past.

In spite of the back-breaking work from dawn to dusk, there
was an urgent satisfaction if not joy about the harvest. It was
the most festive work of the whole year, carried out by entire
families, almost entire villages—for men from other jobs,
thatchers, masons, grooms would join in—and for once there

*A view looking upstream on the River Granta
above Cambridge*

was a bond between farmer and workers in the enthusiasm to bring the harvest home before any break in the weather could endanger it.

It was hard toil, harder perhaps than we can appreciate. Richard Jefferies (who died in **1887**, the year Quinton was exhibiting at the Imperial Jubilee Exhibition—the golden jubilee, that's to say, of Queen Victoria) wrote thus in *Field and Hedgerow*:

> 'More men and more men were put on day by day, and women to bind the sheaves, till the vast field held the village, yet they seemed but a handful buried in the tunnels of the golden mine: they were lost in it like hares, for as the wheat fell, the shocks rose behind them, low tents of corn. Your skin or mine could not have stood the scratching of the straw, which is stiff and sharp, and the burning of the sun which blisters like red hot iron. The whole village lived in the field; a corn-land village is always the most populous, and every rood of land, thereabouts, in a sense, maintains its man. The reaping and the binding up and stacking of the sheaves, and the carting and building of the ricks, and the gleaning, there was something to do for every one, from the very old man down to the very youngest child. . .'.

But of course the urgent zeal of the harvesters wasn't simply altruistic. They weren't out on a mass worship of Ceres. It was partly, or principally, economic. Far better money could be earned at the harvest than at any other time of the year. Five or six good men with their scythes and sickles could cut down a couple of acres in a day and they bargained as best they could with the farmer for a 'reasonable' price for their sweat. Most of the year the labourers worked for a weekly wage; but at harvest-time the arrangement turned to piecework, so much per acre, and the farmer and men were more on equal terms. The harvest simply had to be carted at its peak—and Nature brooks no delay.

Varying from region to region or even village to village, a Lord of the Harvest or a King of the Mowers would be appointed, usually by common consent the best man with a scythe. The second reaper, somewhat bizarrely, was known as the Harvest-lady, while the last man in a gang was often called the Lag-man. It would be up to the Harvest-lord to lead the annual negotiations with the farmer for the wage-rate for that

A delightful vista down Mariner's Score at Lowestoft in Suffolk

particular harvest. Much would depend, for example, on the character of the fields and their accessibility for work and whether the corn had been badly 'laid' by summer storms, 'upstanding' corn being much easier to reap. It was quite a business, wrote Arthur Randell in his *Sixty Years a Fenman* (published in 1966), 'when the harvest men met the farmer to fix the price per acre for tying, shocking and carting. Often they would argue for as much as half a day, but in the end they always came to some agreement and then the farmer would send for some beer to seal the bargain and a start could be made on the work'.

And some farmers would additionally close the deal by giving each man a shilling! It was all reminiscent of Thomas Tusser in the sixteenth century:

> 'Grant harvest lord more by a penie or twoo,
>   to call on his fellowes the better to doo:
> Give gloves to thy reapers, a larges to crie,
>   and dailie to loiterers have a good eie.'

The largess was a gift of money apart from the bargain struck (and the custom of giving gloves continued for a long time). On receiving it, the reapers would cry out three times, 'Halloo largess!', which was the ceremony of 'crying a largess' referred to by Tusser and which still prevailed in parts of East Anglia in the 1890s.

For all the racking work, great was the triumph when the harvest reached its climax. In some regions the ceremony of 'crying the neck' was carried out (there was a considerable correspondence about this in the Plymouth-based *Western Morning News* in 1898), when the reapers would plait the ends of the last sheaf together, tying it with coloured ribbons, then, lifting it triumphantly above their heads and brandishing their sickles, would shout:

> 'We-ha-neck! We-ha-neck!
> Well a-plowed! Well a-sowed!
> We've a -reaped! and we've a-moved!
> Harroosh! Harroosh! Harroosh!'

And then the last golden load was ready, and on top of it the elected Queen of the Harvest dressed in white and bearing that last sheaf decked now with flowers as well as ribbons. She would be accompanied by a bevy of children nestling perilously among the sheaves, and maybe some beer-mazed old grandad stranded there after helping with the loading and holding on for dear life, for there was many a fatal tumble from the height of the laden harvest-wagon. Then the load swayed off through the perfumed dusk to the farmyard, there to be stacked, ready for the thatchers to do their important part and protect the ricks until the time came for threshing.

In some places a special symbolic ceremony was made of the Harvest Home, with people bearing triumphant banners—God giveth all—Speed the plough—Welcome our harvest home—marching at the head, followed by others ringing hand-bells, followed in turn by an enormous wagon-load of corn, drawn by horses also carrying bells strung from the wooden hoops over their backs. All this would be followed by local worthies and many ordinary folk who hadn't taken any part in the harvest but nevertheless appreciated its significance and partook of the general rejoicing.

Likewise important to the workfolk both symbolically and materially was the Harvest Feast. At trestle tables set up in the barn, and served by the farmer and his wife and daughters and maid-servants, the men and women harvesters sat down to a better meal than ever they enjoyed at home during the rest of the year. Inevitably, as the beer flowed and tongues were loosened, somebody would launch into that traditional and interminable old song which made the rafters of many a barn ring:

> 'There was an old dog and he lived at a mill,
> And Bingo was his name, sir,
> B, I, N, G, O,
> Bang her and bop her and kick her and kop her . . .'

And so on, *ad infinitum*, all about a miller who brewed 'right good stingo'. Then the tables and benches were cleared out of the way and, to the accompaniment of fiddle and concertina, the harvesters reeled round the floor in a scene Brueghel would have recognized. It is said that when work resumed its usual

A horse stops to drink at the ford in this colourful picture
of Kersey village, Suffolk

trekking, that it is difficult to envisage how little the country-man had to occupy any spare time he had. Squire and parson had their exclusive sports, hunting, fishing, shooting, in which the farmer joined, though as far as shooting was concerned, it was but a couple of generations since tenant-farmers were first allowed to shoot over the very land they rented and that only with the landlord's sanction. As for the 'hunting' parson, who had sometimes been known to advertise for a living 'where the hunting was good and the duties light', he still existed—even in the mild-mannered form of the Reverend Colwood (in Siegfried Sassoon's *Memoirs of a Fox-hunting Man*) who sat 'well forward in the saddle with the constrained look of a man who rather expects his horse to cross its front legs and pitch him over its head'.

But for most of the workfolk the answer was that they didn't have much spare time—no paid holidays, no days off except Sundays and Bank Holidays (and Queen Victoria's Diamond Jubilee in 1897!), and even then the cowman and the stockman and the groom had to tend their animals. However when workers had sweated out their stint at the 'spud-patch' there was always the village inn, which was often by way of being a club where, while eking out their half-pints, they would wrangle away with the local 'cobbler' (the traditional village 'politician') about Mr Gladstone or the efforts of Joseph Arch to strengthen the national union of farmworkers. After the Reform Act of 1884 when, last of men, male agricultural workers were graci-ously accorded the vote, countrymen were keenly interested in politics, most adhering to the Liberal cause.

Until transport, principally the railways, increased in scope towards the end of the century, lower fares coinciding with slightly higher wages, the village remained much more of a close-knit, separate community. In the 1890s Anderson Graham remarked that a ten-mile journey was an event that kept the labourer in talk for a lifetime. 'Even at this day I know rustics who live within that distance of the sea and yet have never beheld it. A man who had broken bread in two counties was reckoned to have seen a bit of the world.'

So 'leisure activities'—how Quinton's countryman would have scratched his head at that, he'd have been fair 'mazed—

Potter Heigham Bridge in Norfolk: many buildings used to be thatched, including barns, churches and even boathouses

humdrum swing after the Harvest Frolic or Horkey, as it was variously called, the first day of the following week was sometimes known as Sorrowful Monday; a headache and less pay combined to make it so.

Quinton may well have joined in a Harvest Home in one of his villages, but after the turn of the century the 'Feast' began to be abandoned, many farmers giving their work-force a cash handout instead.

But though the Harvest Home has disappeared, that other example of thanksgiving for the bounty of Nature continues— the Harvest Festival, when the village church becomes a veritable temple to the glory of Ceres, and all the good things of the earth, from field and garden, are brought in tribute.

9

We take leisure time so much for granted—indeed, somewhat paradoxically we have a 'leisure industry'—with our paid holidays, easy travel, entertainments of every imaginable kind from opera to bingo and sports ranging from skiing to pony-

Untypically for Quinton, the pines add a touch of menace to this Red-Riding-Hood-like scene at Sheringham Woods in Norfolk

One of Great Yarmouth's famous Rows—the figures of children and a fisherman are particularly delightful

The dramatic Cow and Calf Rocks at Ilkley, Yorkshire,
contrasting with the town below

had to be strictly local, apart from the rare visit to a fair or circus. In the popular nostalgic imagination the rural scene once upon a time was one long round of junketing—from the wassailing of the apple-trees to ensure a good crop to the Midsummer Eve bonfires which were really a pagan hymn to the sun. Some customs lingered on at the turn of the century—and are kept up today—such as beating the bounds, stemming from the days when parish boundaries were of great importance (small boys having their heads bumped on the boundary stones to impress them on their memory); many villages still elected their May Queen and King; while Mothering Sunday is not a modern invention but was practised for many generations, farm-servants being allowed time off to take presents of cakes and frumenty to their mothers.

A cottage at Routh, Yorkshire

Many customs and indeed entertainments were a celebration of work. Plough Monday, the first Monday after Twelfth Day and regarded as the opening of the farming year, was still celebrated; in 1897 the *Daily Mail* carried a report of its being enacted in Warwickshire. A team of men dressed in white smocks and decorated with bunches of ribbon and known as Plough-bullocks, would haul a plough through the village, attended by mountebanks and sword-dancers and morrismen, and needless to say collecting tribute from the onlookers.

A tree-fringed bend in the Yorkshire River Wharfe as it meanders past Bolton Abbey

Unkempt by today's standards, nevertheless these cottages
at Runswick Bay in Yorkshire have an inimitable homely charm

But the most noteworthy example of work and entertainment mingling was the annual ploughing-match that took place in the autumn, that time of year when for a little while the country-man can relax. Even after the introduction of the steam-plough and later on the tractor, while the horse was still paramount, the ploughing-match was an eagerly awaited occasion, with its hint of the far-off past when man first turned a furrow. The whole parish would turn out—strangers from other villages, too—and, together with the real connoisseurs, the carters and horsemen and farm-bailiffs, keenly watched the competing teams plough-ing their 'stetches', a 'stetch' being a parcel of furrows. The horse-brasses would be glinting and jingling in the sunlight, the horses sleek as silk, tails and manes coiffured lovingly, for though primarily it was the ploughing that was being judged, the straight furrow, the rounded headland, there was a prize for the best turned-out team as well. Sometimes there would be a dozen teams competing and in four hours or so two ridges, each of them eleven yards wide, had to be ploughed. Up and down the teams would plod, turning over the stubble whose dim gold steadily disappeared as the ploughs left their rich, dark-brown furrows behind them, the ploughmen intent only on their distant mark of peeled hazel-sticks, silent, serious, almost like priests engaged in some sacred rite, which in effect they were, in their devotion to the earth.

When ancient village sports such as (compulsory) archery, single-stick, wrestling and tilting, with the biff from the quintain for the slow moving, died out, the notorious cross-country football, a violent free-for-all, occasionally took their place. But it was village cricket that gradually came to evoke the whole joyful atmosphere of the English countryside at its best. The sound of bat on ball on the village green or in some meadow loaned by squire or farmer is as characteristic as the sound of church bells or the clink of the blacksmith's hammer on anvil. Cricket has a long history, but it was really in the eighteenth century that it took off and it was remarked that noblemen, gentlemen, parsons and the like were consorting with butchers and cobblers and tinkers and other common men in playing the game.

That indeed was one of the most important aspects of village

FORGE VALLEY
Nʳ SCARBOROUGH

A.R.Q.

A solitary angler enjoys the lush beauty of the Forge Valley
near Scarborough in Yorkshire

Houses clinging to the steep-sided East Cliff in the busy
Yorkshire town of Whitby

THE SHIPWAY,
ROBIN HOOD'S BAY

*This delightful painting of the Shipway at Robin Hood's Bay
in Yorkshire exemplifies Quinton's use of warm colours*

*In an untypical solitary and brooding mood, Quinton here portrays
the Lake District's Kirkstone Pass looking down to Brothers Water*

A fell-side farm, Cumberland

cricket. GM Trevelyan put it nicely thus: 'Squire, farmer, blacksmith and labourer, with their women and children come to see the fun, were at ease together and happy all the summer afternoon. If the French *noblesse* had been capable of playing cricket with their peasants, their chateaux would never have been burnt down'.

One has a vision of Quinton, having cycled through a hot June afternoon, stretched out in the grass at the edge of some flowery meadow, watching the village blacksmith trundling down his cunning leg-breaks and the curate, perhaps, crouching behind the stumps.

In the meantime something of a revolution in people's leisure activities had been taking place. Already as far back as the eighteenth century, doctors had been advising their affluent patients to take the cure at seaside 'watering-places' such as Brighthelmstone—which presently became Brighton. Gentlemen were actually pictured swimming from the beach at Scarborough, while at Margate 'Beale's bathing-machines' were hauled into the water by horses, enabling ladies as well as gentlemen to swim out under cover of a discreet canopy. By the

time of Queen Victoria's accession, Londoners were regularly crowding down to Brighton and Margate, while by 1876 the erstwhile village of Blackpool had acquired the status of a borough, so much had it flourished because of Lancashire factory workers thronging to it.

Quinton's 'watering-places' were the fishing-villages of the south west—Dawlish, Looe, Polperro—where middle-class folk increasingly took their holidays. The fishing families profited accordingly, not only from the resulting trade, but also because many of the visitors took lodgings with them—and the more adventurous enjoyed outings on the sea! Those fishermen (the maritime equivalent of the farm-labourer and the shepherd and the carter) were fortunate in so far as their 'crop' needed neither sowing nor reaping nor tending; but their work was hazardous, the sea was always jealous of its bounty and the work was laborious, too, often taking place at night.

Much of the Cornish fisherman's crop was the teeming pilchards, which were cured, packed in barrels and often exported to Italy. But the 'crown of the the year' was heralded when the cry 'Mackerel's up!' rang out from the 'huer', as he was

*Majestic and tranquil, this Lake District scene shows Ullswater
with Helvellyn in the distance*

*Derwentwater, Cumbria, from Friar's Crag—'so cold was
the temperature and so heavy the clouds' in June when
Quinton bicycled through the Lake District*

AIRA FORCE

A.R.QUINTON

called, an old experienced fisherman who had been stationed on the cliff-top surveying the sea for the first shoal of mackerel showing up dark on the water. Every man-jack in the village would clatter down the cobbled streets to the harbour to launch the seine boats, craft of perhaps thirty feet in length and carrying an encircling net a quarter of a mile long and sixty feet deep. The harvest of the sea was rich in those days, before the advent of freezer-trawler and factory ship that are plundering it recklessly.

This, then, was Quinton's world—with its gull-thronged fishing-harbours, its golden tide-washed beaches, its honeysuckle lanes wandering dreamily into the secret distance, its glinting streams, where swallows hawked the flies and cows stood knee-deep in the water swishing lazy tails, and its cottage gardens whose flowers painted the air with a hundred colours. It was a world which, for all its faults and imperfections, 'kept the noiseless tenor of its way', which we in our abrasive times can perhaps only envy.

Unusually, there are no animals or people in this painting of Aira Force at Ullswater in Cumbria, but the scene is full of movement

INDEX OF ILLUSTRATIONS

In the main part of the book illustrations are grouped by area, starting in the south-east, moving to the south-west and then the Midlands, and ending in the north.

This index lists all watercolours and drawings according to the individual places they portray, with colour-picture page numbers in *italics*. The numbers in brackets are reference numbers for the original postcards produced by J Salmon Ltd.

BOOK REFERENCES

Arch, Joseph *From Ploughman to Parliament* (1898)
Bourne, George *A Farmer's Life* (Cape 1922)
Gibbs, Arthur *A Cotswold Village* (1898)
Graham, Anderson P *The Rural Exodus* (Methuen 1892)
Haggard, H Rider *Rural England* (1906)
Hardy, Thomas *The Woodlanders* (1887), *Tess of the d'Urbervilles* (1891)
Hudson WH *A Shepherd's Life* (1910)
Jefferies, Richard *Field and Hedgerow* (1885)
Randell, Arthur *Sixty Years a Fenman* (Routledge & Kegan Paul 1966)
Street, AG *Farmer's Glory* (Faber 1932)
Thompson, Flora *Lark Rise to Candleford* (Oxford University Press 1945)
Trevelyan, GM *A Social History of England* (Longman 1942)
Wright, Elizabeth Mary *Rustic Speech and Folklore* (Milford 1911)